Tripod Kitty
and the Recipe for Kindness

Enjoy this book and bake the cookies to share kindness.
— Clarice

With Gratitude

Thank you, Mascot Books, for making my experience as a first-time children's book author seamless. I am grateful to every individual at Mascot Books who helped produce this book, many working tirelessly behind the scenes on production, contracting, and finance. I am especially grateful to Nicole, senior production editor, who masterfully coordinated every aspect of this book, from helping to facilitate an illustrator through print production. I am grateful to David for his creative and beautiful illustrations and for capturing the spirit of the real animals upon which this book is based. I am thankful to Jess, senior acquisitions editor, who received and approved my book idea and helped me with the book contract. I am thankful to Shannon, who helped produce a beautiful cover and the layout for the interior book design. I am thankful to Carri in the finance office for ensuring every transaction was efficiently processed. From start to finish, the staff and contractors at Mascot Books helped produce an excellent product.

Sincerely, Clarice Nassif Ransom

To my loving husband, Bill; daughter, Sophia; son, Gabriel; brother, LeRoy; and the good friends and neighbors who encouraged me to write this book.

To those who have gone on to be with the Lord but who influenced me in special ways: My father, Gabriel; mother, Rita; siblings, Clyde, Lillian, and Nancy; and a special high school journalism teacher, Ardys.

"Live in harmony with one another."
Romans 12:16

Thank you, Jesus, for showing us the way and making a path forward for this book.

www.mascotbooks.com

Tripod Kitty and the Recipe for Kindness

©2021 Clarice Nassif Ransom. All Rights Reserved. No part of this publication may be reproduced, stored in a retrieval system or transmitted in any form by any means electronic, mechanical, or photocopying, recording or otherwise without the permission of the author.

For more information, please contact:
Mascot Books
620 Herndon Parkway #320
Herndon, VA 20170
info@mascotbooks.com

Library of Congress Control Number: 2021906134

CPSIA Code: PRV0421A
ISBN-13: 978-1-64543-909-7

Printed in the United States of America

Tripod Kitty
and the Recipe for Kindness

Clarice Nassif Ransom

Illustrated by David Gnass

Hi, my name is Orie.

Everyone now knows me as "Tripod Kitty," as I am a three-legged cat because my front right leg was amputated due to cancer. Before, I was handsome and athletic. After my leg was amputated, I did not look the same or move as fast. I had to learn to use three legs instead of four. I do most activities like I did before, only now with a hop. It was hard at first. I had to accept my new self. Others had to accept that I am different. I want you to be inspired by my story, especially if you are struggling with not being like everyone else for whatever reason. In this book, find out about how I overcame cancer and learned the recipe for kindness.

Chapter 1:
Last Day of School

Orie is a handsome and popular kitty. He is known as the fastest runner, quickest tree climber, and sneakiest bug catcher at Ardys Creek Elementary School.

Orie's good friends are Ding the dog, Sammy the squirrel, and Tommy the turtle. Everyone loves Orie, except for the crow brothers, Kah and Hah. They like to pick on Orie.

Ms. Ardys is everyone's favorite teacher at Ardys Creek Elementary School.

Ms. Ardys makes all the children feel special, even Kah and Hah. Every morning at the beginning of the school day, she says,

"Everyone is welcome in my class."

Today is the last day of school. Everyone is excited for summer break to begin—even Ms. Ardys.

As the last school bell rings, Ms. Ardys says to all the children, "Have a wonderful summer. Please remember our class motto: Live in harmony with each other." As she says these words, Ms. Ardys looks directly at Kah and Hah. Ms. Ardys knows they are not nice to Orie.

As Orie, Ding, Sammy, and Tommy are walking on the path home, Kah and Hah are flying high above the others. Everyone is now out of Ms. Ardys' line of sight.

"Let's pull Orie's tail," says Kah.

"Yeah, Orie is such a show-off, strutting around like he is better than everyone," says Hah.

Kah and Hah wait until Sammy the squirrel is in her tree house and Tommy the turtle is in his mud hut. Ding and Orie are crossing

the big, blue bridge. They are neighbors and best friends. They don't suspect anything as they walk together, tails in the air, chatting and sharing happy thoughts about summer break with each other.

"You distract Ding," says Kah.

Hah snickers, nods in agreement, and then dives at Ding's face, making sure his tail feathers touch the tip of Ding's nose.

This angers Ding, and he chases Hah, who laughs as he flies high in the sky out of Ding's reach.

Meanwhile, Kah swoops down and pulls Orie's tail, snatching a few hairs in his beak as he flies away.

"Ouch!" yells Orie, jumping up with both front paws aimed at the sky, claws ready to grasp Kah. "I am going to get even with you, Kah."

Kah, already high above in the trees, laughs and says, "I would like to see you try. You can't catch us, and we will be gone for the entire summer visiting our aunt."

Kah and Hah disappear quickly over the horizon.

Ding says to Orie, "Ignore them. They are not worth our time. We have too much to do this summer to worry about them."

Ding and Orie continue on the path home.

Chapter 2:
Summer Break and Overcoming Cancer

"I love summer," Orie says to Ding.

"Me, too—we can play together every day," says Ding.

For the first month of summer, Orie and Ding are inseparable. They do everything together—go to parties, host barbeques, swim in the creek, and watch movies under the stars.

Then, one morning when Orie is outside playing by himself near where his mother is gardening, Orie feels a sharp pain in his right front leg. Orie starts to limp and can no longer play.

"Mom, my leg hurts, and I can't walk," Orie cries as he sits down on a tree stump next to his mother.

"You have a large lump on your leg," says Orie's mother. "We need to take you to the doctor."

Orie's mother and father rush Orie to the hospital. At the hospital, Dr. Zachie runs several tests and discovers that Orie has bone cancer.

"Orie, the lump on your leg is a rare form of bone cancer," Dr. Zachie explains. "The good news is that you can overcome this type of cancer and live a long life. However, we will need to remove your right front leg to prevent the cancer from spreading. You will be a three-legged cat, but you will be able to do everything you used to do, just in a different way."

Orie bursts into tears. Orie's mother and father wrap their paws around Orie to comfort him.

"Orie, we love you and are here for you always," says Orie's father. "You need to have this surgery."

Orie is sent to a hospital room, and his surgery is scheduled for the next day. Orie's father and mother decide to spend the night in the hospital room with Orie.

"Let's say a prayer and ask God to bless Dr. Zachie and his staff for a successful surgery to remove all of Orie's cancer," says Orie's father.

"I also want to pray for Orie to recover and to be a happy kitty," says Orie's mother.

Orie, sad and scared, is comforted by the prayers and by his parents staying with him in the hospital room.

The next day, Orie has his surgery.

When the procedure is over, Dr. Zachie comes into the waiting room where Orie's parents are sitting. "We removed all of the cancer, and Orie will be fine," explains Dr. Zachie. "Orie will need plenty of rest for

the first few days. Try to get him to eat right away—this will help build his strength. After that, he can start to move around—the sooner he starts getting back to normal, the better."

Orie's parents are grateful to Dr. Zachie and give him a big hug. Orie stays in the hospital for one day after his surgery and then goes home with his parents, a bit groggy and in a lot of pain.

The first few days of recovery at home are tough. Orie has to take a lot of medicine and sleeps for most of the day. After a week, Ding asks if he can visit Orie. Orie's parents think Ding will be the best medicine to help Orie feel better. When Ding arrives, he sees the sadness in Orie's eyes and demeanor.

"Hi, Orie," says Ding. "I brought you some kitty treats and our favorite card game."

Orie immediately perks up at the sight of Ding. Ding stays by Orie's side for the rest of the summer, helping him to recover from cancer.

Orie hops instead of walks as he trails Ding down to the creek to drink fresh water. Orie learns to run on three legs by chasing after Ding as they play tag. Orie even catches a few bugs!

At the end of August, Orie is physically ready to go back to school, and Ding is a pillar of strength for Orie.

Chapter 3:
Back to School

On the first day of school, Orie is afraid.

"I am different," Orie cries to Ding. "I don't look the same. I can't run as fast. No one will like me."

"You are special," says Ding. "I am proud of you, Orie, the three-legged cat. I call you the Tripod Kitty. You never let cancer or having three legs instead of four defeat you."

Orie is not convinced. He wonders, *What will everyone think? How will they treat me?* Orie is sad. He thinks, *Kah and Hah did not like me before. Now that I hop instead of run, they will pick on me even more.*

Orie and Ding walk to school. Kah and Hah

fly overhead, and they spot Orie and Ding.

"Let's swoop down and scare Orie," says Kah.

"Okay—like we did on the last day of school. I will try to pull Orie's tail, but this time, you should peck at his ear," says Hah.

When Kah and Hah see Orie hopping, they laugh.

"What happened to you?" Kah swoops down and pecks at Orie's ear.

"Don't you know how to walk?" Hah swoops down from the other side and pulls Orie's tail.

Orie tries to hop away, but starts to cry.

Ding becomes angry when he sees how Kah and Hah mistreat Orie. He growls and snarls at them.

Kah and Hah know they are in trouble. Ding starts to chase them, but Kah and Hah escape as they fly above the others.

Sammy the squirrel climbs down from her tree house and sees everything. "Why are you crying, Orie?" Sammy asks. Then, she sees that Orie is missing his right front leg. Sammy is not sure what to say.

Ding steps in and says, "Orie had cancer, and he lost his leg. But Orie is the same friend and kitty we love. He just can't run like he used to. But, he can hop, and he can catch bugs."

Sammy is quiet. She gives Orie a hug.

Tommy the turtle comes hobbling up to Orie, Ding, and Sammy. Tommy knows what it is like to be different. He is slow. Many times, Tommy is left behind on the playground. Orie used to leave Tommy out of games because he said Tommy was too slow. Kah and Hah pecked at Tommy's shell last year for no reason. So, Tommy knows what it feels like to be picked on. Tommy's heart breaks when he sees Orie crying.

Tommy does not say anything, but he sits next to Orie. This is Tommy's way to say that he stands with Orie. Kah and Hah swoop

back down so they will not be late for class.

Ding barks, "Why don't you leave us alone? We do not like you."

Sammy, who is usually kind to everyone, agrees. "You are mean and made Orie cry."

Kah says, "Orie always acts like he is better than us."

Hah agrees, "Orie used to leave Tommy out of games because he thinks Tommy is too slow. He used to leave us out of everything because he does not like us—because we fly instead of walk or run."

Meanwhile, Ms. Ardys observes everything from behind a big rock. She knows that the kids are being mean to each other, and this makes her sad. Ms. Ardys realizes she needs a recipe for kindness to teach the children to be nice and to respect each other.

I have an idea, Ms. Ardys thinks. *This will help everyone come together.*

Orie, Ding, Sammy, Tommy, Kah, and Hah arrive in their classroom at Ardys Creek

Elementary School. Everyone is a bit unsettled because of what happened on the way to school that morning.

Ms. Ardys steps into the classroom and addresses all the children.

"Welcome back to school, everyone," says Ms. Ardys. "It is great to see you. Who remembers our class motto?"

Sammy raises her hand. "I do. Live in harmony with one another, and treat others the way you want them to treat you. I added that last part because I think we need it. We need to be nice to each other."

"Very good, Sammy," says Ms. Ardys.

Orie thinks, *Gee, I have not been so nice to Tommy. Last year, I left him out of games because I thought he was slow. Maybe I do ignore Kah and Hah and make them feel unwelcome.*

Kah whispers to Hah, "Why does Ms. Ardys bring up this motto all the time? Can't she find something better to talk about?" Hah nods in agreement.

Tommy is happy that Ms. Ardys mentions the class motto, and he likes Sammy's addition about treating others the way you want them to treat you. He hopes everyone will follow it.

Ding is not listening. He is thinking about how he is going to get even with Kah and Hah.

Ms. Ardys begins the day's lessons. First, the class adds and subtracts numbers. Then, the class reads out loud. When the reading time is over, Ms. Ardys announces that the students can go home early. Everyone is excited. Then, Ms. Ardys gives the class a strange homework assignment.

"I want each of you to bring in an item tomorrow," says Ms. Ardys. "Here is the sign-up sheet. Sign your name next to an ingredient and bring it in for our lesson. We are going to bake my Aunt Sophia's chocolate chip cookies. Instead of coming to Ardys Creek Elementary School for class, come to my home—the small, yellow cottage next to the rock where there are a lot of trees. I will supply the tools you need to bake cookies, and I will contribute sugar and molasses. You will supply the rest of the ingredients."

"Yum," say Sammy and Ding. "This is going to be fun." Sammy signs up to bring flour, and Ding signs up to bring eggs.

Kah and Hah are excited. They love chocolate chip cookies. Kah signs up to bring chocolate chips, and Hah signs up to bring salt and baking soda.

Tommy signs up to bring butter. Orie signs up to bring vanilla extract, almond extract, and cinnamon.

"I can't wait until tomorrow," Orie says to Tommy as all the children exit the schoolyard to go home. Tommy nods in agreement.

Kah and Hah have crowing lessons, so they don't pick on anyone as they rush to their mother's music studio.

Chapter 4:
Kindness Recipe

The next morning, Orie and Ding are the first to arrive at Ms. Ardys' house with ingredients in hand. All the other children arrive within minutes of Orie and Ding and are ready to have fun and to eat chocolate chip cookies.

"Welcome to my home, everyone," says Ms. Ardys. "Before we do anything, I want everyone to wash their hands with soap and warm water. It is very important to keep clean when you bake."

After all the children finish washing and drying their hands, Ms. Ardys asks them to sit around the big table in her kitchen and to place their ingredients on the table.

"Thank you for bringing in all the ingredients to bake my Aunt Sophia's chocolate chip cookies," says Ms. Ardys. "Ding, you brought in eggs. Who here would like to eat raw eggs?" asks Ms. Ardys.

"Yuck. That does not sound like it would taste good," Hah says. All the children agree.

"Hah, you brought in salt and baking soda. Who would like to taste a teaspoon of salt or a teaspoon of baking soda by itself?" asks Ms. Ardys.

"That would taste horrible," say Sammy and Orie, almost at the same time. All the children agree.

"I brought in butter," says Tommy. "That is fine to taste by itself." Not all the children agree, especially Ding, who says raw butter makes his tummy upset.

"I brought in chocolate chips," says Kah, a bit proud, "and everybody likes chocolate chips." Everyone agrees.

"What about vanilla extract, almond

extract, and cinnamon—would you eat those ingredients by themselves?" asks Ms. Ardys.

"No way," says Orie. All the children agree, shaking their heads no.

"How about sugar and molasses—would you eat those ingredients by themselves?" asks Ms. Ardys.

Tommy says, "Yes!" But the rest of the children say, "No."

Sammy adds, "Too much sugar by itself makes my nose twitch. I tried it once. Molasses is too spicy by itself."

"So, what I am hearing from all of you is that many of the ingredients we are going to use to bake chocolate chip cookies today would not taste good on their own," says Ms. Ardys.

"Yes," agree all the children.

"That is a very interesting observation," says Ms. Ardys. "Now, let's start our baking project. I need everyone to work together. Some of you will measure the ingredients.

Some of you will stir the ingredients together."

Ms. Ardys splits the children into two groups. Kah, Orie, and Tommy have to measure and mix the flour, salt, baking soda, and cinnamon together. Hah, Ding, and Sammy have to melt the butter and then mix the melted butter with the eggs, sugar, molasses, vanilla, and almond extract.

"Now, I want both groups to combine all of your ingredients into this big bowl," says Ms. Ardys. "Once that is done, we will each take a turn stirring all of the ingredients together. Ding, we will start with you. Stir the mixture with the wooden spoon three times. Then, hand the wooden spoon to someone else until everyone gets a turn stirring the cookie dough. Stir the dough three circles per child. I am counting on all of you to work together to ensure everyone has a turn."

While the children are busy stirring the cookie mixture, Ms. Ardys clears the dirty dishes, heats the oven, and brings cookie sheets over to the big table.

"Now, how does the cookie mixture look?" asks Ms. Ardys.

"Wonderful—but it smells even better," says Tommy with a big grin on his face. "And everyone stirred the dough three times like you asked. I was the last one to stir the cookie dough."

Ms. Ardys is a little surprised that Tommy is the first to speak up.

"Well, Tommy, thank you for sharing your thoughts," says Ms. Ardys. "Now, let's bake those cookies so we can eat them."

Ms. Ardys again assigns the children different tasks. "Tommy, Sammy, and Hah, I want you to work together to scoop the cookie mix onto the baking pans and bring the baking pans to me to put into the oven. It will be your responsibility to bake the cookies.

"Kah and Ding, I want you to wash, dry, and put away all of the dirty dishes I left in the sink," says Ms. Ardys. "Orie, I want you to help me set the table and pour glasses of milk for everyone."

Kah sees that Orie may need help pouring the milk. Orie is struggling with holding the milk bottle steady enough to pour the milk into the glasses on the table.

"I am going to help Orie pour the milk," Kah says to Ding as they finish drying the dishes and cleaning the sink.

Ms. Ardys is touched by Kah's gesture of kindness and watches Kah help Orie pour the milk. Orie is grateful to Kah for helping him. Orie was secretly worried that he would be unable to pour the milk without spilling it everywhere.

The kitchen is a happy place. Everyone works together and gets along. The air smells of chocolate and cinnamon. As soon as the first batch of cookies is done, Ms. Ardys pulls the pans out of the oven to cool. Everyone crowds around.

"Yum! This smells so good," says Tommy. "I can hardly wait to eat one."

Kah and Hah say, "Yes, let's eat."

Ms. Ardys asks all of the children to sit around the table, and she will serve the cookies.

"I want you to sit by someone you normally do not sit next to at lunch," Ms. Ardys instructs the children.

Orie sits next to Kah. Ding sits on the other side of Orie, next to Sammy the squirrel. Sammy sits next to Ms. Ardys and shares a chocolate chip cookie with Hah, who sits next to Tommy the turtle.

"Now, I want to thank all of you for making a wonderful batch of cookies," says Ms. Ardys. "Let's eat."

Everyone gobbles the cookies. As the children are eating, Ms. Ardys asks, "How do the cookies taste?"

"They are the best cookies I have ever eaten," says Kah, and Hah agrees.

Ding and Tommy say, "Yummy."

Sammy says, "They are gooey and delicious."

"I never knew it was this much fun to make cookies that are so tasty," says Orie.

"How did it feel to work together?" asks Ms. Ardys.

"We had fun and were nice to each other," says Kah. Everyone agrees.

"That is a good observation, Kah," says Ms. Ardys. "There is something else I want you to think about," Ms. Ardys continues. "The ingredients by themselves do not taste good—no one wants to eat raw eggs, baking soda, or flour, do you?" asks Ms. Ardys.

"No," everyone says all at once.

"But, what happens when you mix all the ingredients together to make and to bake the cookie dough?" asks Ms. Ardys.

"We have the most delicious cookies to eat," says Orie, and everyone agrees. "And we have fun working together."

"Very good, Orie," says Ms. Ardys. "You have learned a huge lesson. Individually, others are different from you. Some are salty, or bitter, or sweet, but when we come together and we treat others the way we want to be treated, we make an excellent mixture. This is the recipe for kindness."

Kah and Hah realize they are mean to the other children because they feel hurt that no one likes them. They also realize that they made Orie feel really bad in spite of Orie overcoming cancer and living as a three-legged cat—different from the rest.

Kah and Hah say, "Will you forgive us for being mean? We are sorry, Orie. We admire you for recovering from cancer and coming back to school a three-legged cat, or as Ding says, the Tripod Kitty. We are sorry, Tommy, for pecking at you."

Tommy nods and smiles.

Orie says, "Will you all forgive me for leaving you out, especially Tommy, Kah, and

Hah? I did not realize how I was being mean. Now I understand what it is like to be different. I really appreciate everyone."

Ding and Sammy are so happy. They say, "We want everyone to be friends."

Tommy says, "Let's eat more cookies!"

Everyone hugs each other, and the kitchen fills with laughter and animal chatter as the children munch on more cookies.

Ms. Ardys sits back and watches how one, simple activity—making Aunt Sophia's chocolate chip cookies—brings everyone together to work in harmony and treat each other with kindness and respect. *This is indeed a recipe for kindness,* thinks Ms. Ardys.

When class is done for the day, Ms. Ardys sends each child home with a package of cookies and her Aunt Sophia's chocolate chip cookie recipe.

"Making my Aunt Sophia's chocolate chip cookies may be the most valuable life lesson I can teach you, kids," Ms. Ardys says as she gives each child a hug goodbye for the day. "Always remember to live in harmony with each other and treat others the way you would want them to treat you."

> **Aunt Sophia's Chocolate Chip Cookie Kindness Checklist**
>
> - Live in harmony with each other
> - Treat others the way you would want them to treat you
> - Accept and appreciate differences

Chapter 5:
Bake Aunt Sophia's Chocolate Chip Cookies

Ingredients:
- 1 teaspoon baking soda
- 1 teaspoon salt
- 2 ¼ cup all-purpose baking flour
- 2 teaspoons cinnamon
- 1 cup (2 sticks) butter, partially melted
- 2 tablespoons of molasses (more or less to your taste)
- 1 ½ cups granulated sugar (more or less to your taste)
- 2 large eggs
- 1 teaspoon vanilla extract
- 1 teaspoon almond extract
- 12-16 ounces semisweet chocolate chips

Directions:
1. Preheat oven to 375 degrees Fahrenheit.
2. Combine baking soda, salt, flour, and cinnamon in a medium bowl and set to the side.
3. Then, stir (or beat with a mixer) the butter, molasses, and sugar until combined. Add one egg at a time, then add the vanilla and almond extract (can stir or beat with a mixer).
4. Gradually add the flour mixture. Once fully combined, fold in the chocolate chips.
5. Bake 6-10 minutes or until golden brown.

About the Author

Clarice learns from every experience in life. Some of the characters in this book are inspired by real people and animals. Ms. Ardys is based on Clarice's mother and a special high school journalism teacher. Both of these extraordinary women were wise, kind, and strong. They sparked Clarice's creativity and writing capabilities. Orie and Ding are based on Clarice's family's pets. Clarice's cat lost his front right limb to cancer, and her dog was the best friend who helped the cat recover. Aunt Sophia's chocolate chip cookie recipe is courtesy of Clarice's daughter. Clarice is blessed to have a loving family and many treasured friends. Clarice hopes you enjoy this book and encourages you to bake the cookies as a way to connect with others, especially if they are different from you.